Dance of the Sacred Circle

A Native American Tale

Adapted and Illustrated by
KRISTINA RODANAS

Little, Brown and Company
Boston New York Toronto London

For David, who helped me find the dragonfly and follow the eagle
Special thanks to Tom Gunning, Janice Hank, and Kateri Waystack

First Edition

Library of Congress Cataloging-in-Publication Data
Rodanas, Kristina.
    Dance of the sacred circle : a Native American tale
adapted and illustrated by Kristina Rodanas. — 1st ed.
        p.   cm.
    Summary: A Blackfoot legend about a young boy who goes looking for
the Great Chief of the Sky in hopes of finding help for his starving
tribe and is rewarded with a special gift, the first horse.
    ISBN 0-316-75358-0
    ISBN 0-316-91155-0 (UK pb)
    1. Sihasapa Indians — Legends. [1. Sihasapa Indians — Legends.
2. Indians of North America — Legends. 3. Horses — Folklore.]
I. Title.
E99.S53R63   1994
398.2'089'975. — dc20
[398.2]
[E]   93-19626

10 9 8 7 6 5 4 3 2 1

SC

Published simultaneously in Canada by Little, Brown & Company (Canada) Limited and in Great Britain by Little, Brown and Company (UK) Limited

Paintings done in colored pencil over watercolor wash.
Text set in Palatino by Typographic House and display lines set in Stentor and Palatino.

Printed in Hong Kong

Author's Note

Dance of the Sacred Circle was inspired by a Blackfeet myth first published in Robert Vaughn's *Then and Now; Or Thirty-Six Years in the Rockies* (Minneapolis: Tribune Printing Company, 1900). In the tradition of storytelling, I have told the tale in my own way. It is intended to speak of the interconnection of all things in Nature and of the common bond that unites us all.

Ages ago, in a land as endless
as the sky, there lived a tribe of
people who roamed the prairies
in search of buffalo. With only
friendly dogs to help them carry
their belongings, following the
buffalo from place to place was
difficult. But the buffalo's meat
made them strong, and its shaggy
fur kept them warm. From its
tough hide, they raised sturdy
tipis that stood in a circle and
reached toward the sun.

Gradually, the great herds
became scarce. Brave hunters
scouted in all directions but
returned home empty-handed.
When the people had eaten all of
the dried meat they had stored,
they began to go hungry, and fear
stalked through the camp.

One boy in particular suffered from the lack of food. He had no parents and no name, and although the tribe cared for him as best they could, he often went without. Many thought he was strange, for he seldom spoke and his cheek was marked by a long, ugly scar.

Though his lips were often closed, the boy's eyes and ears were always open. One night, when the chiefs met to discuss the tribe's situation, he drew near to hear their powerful songs and watch as they passed the sacred pipe. By a glowing fire, he listened to their stories.

The old ones spoke of the Great Chief in the Sky, whose breath gave life to all the world. They said he lived in a wonderful land far above the stars, where the prairies were always green and everyone lived forever.

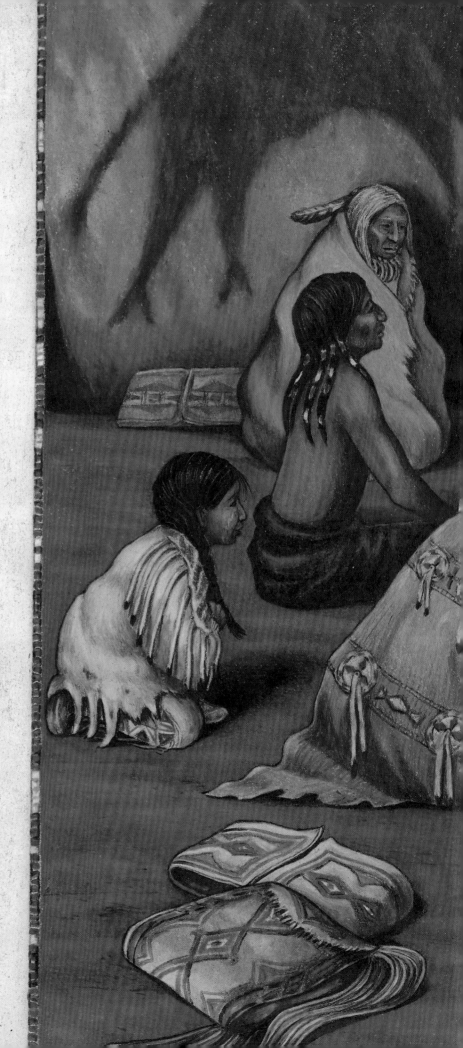

The old ones' words sounded beautiful to the boy, and he wondered if the Great Chief would help his people find the buffalo. He decided to visit him and ask for his assistance. "He must live at the top of the highest mountain," he thought, "where Eagle makes her nest."

The boy left camp silently, heading for the distant mountains. He walked over miles of lonely prairie and swam across a wide river. Each day at dawn, he faced the rising sun and asked the morning wind to guide him.

One evening he reached the foothills at last. Too tired to go on, he fell asleep in the shadow of the tallest peak. He dreamed that he soared high above the clouds and followed a trail of stars to the Great Chief's lodge.

The boy awoke to the sound of thunder. Shivering, he looked up and saw an old man walking toward him. He wore a robe of white buckskin that glowed like the sun, and eagle feathers trailed from his hair.

The Great Chief laid his hand on the boy's shoulder. His face was wise and gentle. "I have watched you these past days," he said. "You are brave to come so far. I wish to give you a special gift. Now, then, my son, bring me some mud."

The boy did as he was told. The Great Chief knelt on the grass and began to shape the mud with his hands. As he worked, he sang strange words, and the wet earth took form under his fingers. The child stared in surprise as the mud shape grew and grew until it became as large as a dog.

The Great Chief stepped back from his work and beckoned the boy to him. Then he called together a sacred council of all the trees in the forest, the birds in the air, and the animals that roamed the plains. They all came and gathered around the pair.

"I am making a special gift for this boy," the Great Chief told them. "It will be an animal for him to ride. It will carry his burdens, and it will help his people find the buffalo. I ask that you give something special of yourselves to help make this creature perfect."

The council kept silent while they considered the Great Chief's request. Pine Tree was the first to respond. Bowing low, she whispered, "Great Chief, your work is good, but it has no tail. It needs a tail to be perfect, and I will gladly give it one."

Then Fir Tree shook his heavy boughs and said, "The animal's neck is bare. I will give it a magnificent mane. The boy will be able to grasp it to steady himself while he rides. That will make it perfect."

Turtle crept forward. "Its feet are very soft," she observed. "I will harden them to make its step sure. Then it will be perfect." The boy watched as Turtle slowly circled around the strange animal.

Like an arrow, Hawk soared overhead, startling the others. She spiraled downward and landed at the boy's feet with a great flurry of wings. "Great Chief," she cried, "your work is good, but it is not yet perfect. The animal must be swift if it is to race the mighty buffalo. I will grant it speed." Hawk flew into the air and glided in a smooth circle above the creature.

Then Elk leaped from the crowd and pranced about the mud creature. "Your work is good, Great Chief," he called, "but it is too small for the boy to ride. I am very large. Allow me to make it bigger!"

A long, low howl echoed on the wind. A little afraid, the boy shrank behind the Great Chief as out from the shadows trotted Wolf. "The creature must have courage to withstand the thunder of the buffalo's hooves," he growled. "This I will provide." Then he followed Elk into the circle.

Fawn stepped carefully in front of the crowd. "Great Chief," she said shyly, "your work is good, but the animal must be gentle if its rider is to trust it. I will make it so."

Fawn scurried after the others. The boy's eyes widened with wonder as they all danced around the earthen statue and bestowed their gifts. Like a swirling stream, the rest of the council joined the circle. All moved together as magic flowed among them.

Then the Great Chief raised his painted shield, signaling an end to the celebration. At once the dancing stopped, and the council members stepped back to admire their creation. A beautiful horse stood motionless before them.

The Great Chief walked up to the horse and stroked her nose. He blew softly into each nostril. The horse began to breathe, then slowly stretched her neck. She lifted one leg, then the next, and took her first wobbling steps.

Turning to the boy, the Great Chief announced, "The horse is now perfect. Take her, my son, and treasure her always."

"Great Chief," the boy said in a low voice, "the gift you have made for me is a wonderful thing. But I wish to give something of myself so that it will be complete."

The council members backed away as the Great Chief considered the boy's request. With a slow nod, he gave his consent.

The boy approached the horse, now so full of life. Tenderly, he touched her smooth coat and looked up into her soft eyes. Then he took her head in his hands and laid his scarred cheek on the horse's nose. When he raised his head, a blaze of white streaked the dark fur like a shooting star in the night sky.

The Great Chief lifted the child onto the horse's back. The boy grasped her mane, and together they began the long journey home.

At first the boy was frightened, but as they traveled across the plains he learned how to guide the horse with his legs and a murmur of his voice. When they came to the edge of the wide river, he urged the mare into the rushing current. As they swam toward the opposite shore, the river began to bubble and foam. All over the surface of the water, horses' heads began to appear. There were hundreds and hundreds of them, of many different colors. When they reached land, the horses leaped from the water and galloped wildly up the bank.

Amazed, the boy continued on with the prancing herd following behind.

When the boy entered the camp, the tribe drew back in fear from the strange animals. But the horses were beautiful, and they seemed gentle. When the boy explained that the new animals were a gift from the Great Chief, the people's fear quickly changed to excitement.

One by one, the hunters picked out the strongest and bravest horses. With the boy's help, they learned how to maneuver their steeds with grace and quickness. Soon they were ready to ride over craggy hills and across wide valleys, to the faraway country where the buffalo grazed.

On the day of the next hunt, the boy accompanied the hunters as far as a distant mountain range, then rode off alone. He guided his horse to the top of the highest peak. From there he watched as the hunters approached the buffalo.

With the swift animals beneath them, the brave men charged into the stampeding herd. Arrows flew and many buffalo fell. As a great cloud of dust rose, the boy's gaze lifted to the place where the sky touches the earth. He thanked the Great Chief, and all those who had helped make the horse perfect.

At the end of the hunt, there was plenty of buffalo meat for everyone, and the people's hunger ended. For many years to come they would live in happiness, and the boy would have an important place in the tribe as keeper of the Great Chief's precious gift.